AN
ORCA
YOUNG
READER

Flight from Big Tangle

Anita Daher

ORCA BOOK PUBLISHERS

National Library of Canada Cataloguing in Publication Data
Daher, Anita, 1965 -

Flight from Big Tangle

"An Orca young reader"

ISBN 1-55143-234-X

1. Airtankers (Forest fire control)--Juvenile fiction. I. Title.

PS8557.A35F54 2002   jC813'.6   C2002-910872-1

PZ7.D145FI 2002

Library of Congress Control Number: 2002109764

Summary: Lost in the forest as a fire rages, Kaylee finds her way
home only to discover that she must overcome her fear of flying
and pilot a floatplane to safety.

Orca Book Publishers gratefully acknowledges the support of
its publishing programs provided by the following agencies:
the Department of Canadian Heritage, the Canada Council
for the Arts, and the British Columbia Arts Council.

Design by Christine Toller
Cover & interior illustrations by Stephen McCallum
Printed and bound in Canada

IN CANADA	IN THE UNITED STATES
Orca Book Publishers	Orca Book Publishers
PO Box 5626, Station B	PO Box 468
Victoria, BC Canada	Custer, WA USA
V8R 6S4	98240-0468

04 03 02 • 5 4 3 2 1

Hugs and heartfelt thanks to Jim and the girls, my cheerleaders and challengers; my editor Maggie, the most courageous woman I've never met; Dr. Cindy Shmon, Associate Professor Small Animal Surgery, Western College of Veterinary Medicine; Dan Cesar for his study of leg-hold traps and their perils; Don Johnson and the staff of the Canadian Bushplane Heritage Centre in Sault Ste. Marie; the Yellowknife writing community, with a special nod to Jamie Bastedo and his book *Shield Country*; Tim Wynne-Jones, a man whose writing is as beautiful as he is; my mother, for making me believe all is possible; and my father, for giving me the words to fly.

*Courage is the price that life exacts
for granting peace.*

Amelia Earhart
1897 - 1937

Chapter One

The cabin of the small floatplane was hot, yet Kaylee shivered. Her head pounded. Her stomach loop-de-looped as if she were on a Ferris wheel. If her mom didn't land the plane now, Kaylee was going to throw up. If anything, this time was worse than the last.

"You're looking a bit green, Kaylee," her mother said into her headset mike.

Kaylee pushed her own mike to the side and nodded weakly, her long black hair damp and sticking to her cheek and neck.

It had never been like this when Dad was around.

"Okay, I get the picture," Mom said, and turned the nose of the floatplane back toward the tiny, bottlenecked bay they called home. Kaylee pressed her forehead to the window, gazing past the main body of the lake below toward the thick boreal forest beyond: an army of jack pine and poplar, tamarack and birch, warriors with green wool tunics tattered and worn from battle, each leaning on the next for support. The wild, wild woods went on past forever, and she and her mom lived smack in the middle of the whole tangled mess of them.

Kaylee breathed deeply — in through her nose, out through her mouth. Within minutes they were back over the narrow channel that joined Booker Bay to the larger lake.

A year ago Kaylee had loved flying, never got sick from it, and she desperately wished that time back. Ever since she could remember, when the leaves began to turn, she and her parents would fly their small float plane south to St. Lucia, a hot, fertile island on the eastern edge of the Caribbean sea. Dad would make it an adventure, taking a different route each time, stopping along the way in the United States, in places they had never been.

St. Lucia was home for Dad, though it wasn't where he was born — the Donally family had immigrated there from Ireland when he was eight. Papa Donally worked for the Air and Sea Ports Authority and would often visit St. Lucia's two airports. Dad went with him whenever he wasn't in school, watching through chain-link fencing as planes landed and took off, hanging out in briefing rooms where pilots filed their flight plans. No one was surprised when he grew up to be a pilot.

He was flying a charter for a tourist company when he met Mom. She had been sent to Florida by the provincial government for special flight training — this was before she started flying the big CL-215 water bombers — and decided to enjoy a vacation in the Caribbean before heading back home. Dad joked that she had liked his "air frame," and that the rest was history.

Living in two countries wasn't a problem for Mom and Dad. After they got married, they'd fly people and freight around St. Lucia and other nearby islands from September to May. When the rainy season arrived in the Caribbean, the forest fire season was just beginning in Canada, so north they'd go to fly water bombers. They said that they flew for hire and for fire, that flying was in their blood and probably in Kaylee's too.

"Okay, Hon, hang on ..."

The nausea tightened to a hard nut in the pit of Kaylee's belly as her mom angled the plane nose down on short final. Her heart pounded in her ears; her chest

and neck burned. She closed her eyes, unable to watch the final moments. As soon as the pontoons slapped the surface the nut dissolved, and she opened her eyes.

"Thanks, Mom," Kaylee said, staring at a scrape on her knee, wishing it had been better this time.

Mom didn't get many days off work, but when she did Kaylee would sometimes ask if they could try a short flight. Mom must have known that lately Kaylee would rather do anything than climb into an airplane, but always said yes. Kaylee was determined to get past this recent and unexpected fear. She had to.

Sometimes when her mom was at work, she would sit alone in the plane listening to the water lap against the pontoons and dock, her heart thumping against the wall of her chest. She'd remember the way it used to be, soaring past candy-floss clouds, gazing at a patchwork land below. She'd force her pulse to slow by concentrating on her breathing — sucking air in through her nose and slowly out through her mouth.

"Don't worry about it, Kaylee," her mother said gently, maneuvering the plane toward their private dock where a tri-colored basset hound sat watching them, his tail thumping. "We'll keep trying. I'm sure it will pass someday."

"I know, Mom," Kaylee said, but she didn't.

Chapter Two

The summer day sparkled. A few wisps of high cirrus cloud feathered a bluebell sky. The sun was a pot of white, bright and hot. She peered up at it through her fingers, her eyes watering. The cool of the northern forest beckoned as always. After helping her mom secure the Cessna, she grabbed her walking stick from the back deck and took off into the woods with her favorite friend.

"Where are you going to be?" her mom called after her.

"Red Sector!" she yelled, trotting up the path after her disappearing basset hound.

Kaylee always knew exactly where she was going, but using their own special code made her mom feel better. A few years ago their neighbor Jack had brought them a map showing most of the hiking trails in the area. They had taken a ruler, and divided the map into four sections, assigning a different color to each. Whenever she went hiking, she picked her sector, and called out a color — or pinned a raven's feather to it if her mom wasn't around. It was much easier to pick a color than to try and explain a set of paths.

They lived in Blue Sector — the upper left corner of the map. Paths in that corner mostly led from cottages to the bay on the right or the other way to the highway and beyond. The highway cut straight north along the middle of the map before slicing through Blue Sector, dividing it like pie pieces as it curved around Booker Bay toward the main lake further east.

Yellow Sector was directly south. Walking paths hooked up with wider snowmobile paths used in winter. They'd take you along the edge of Misto Lake all the way to town if you followed them long enough.

Red Sector was west, just across the highway from Yellow, and it was her favorite. There was a path in Red Sector that led to a patch of sand dunes. It was easy to lie back in the warm sand, squint at the sun, and imagine that she was back on St. Lucia.

Green Sector sat in the northwest corner of the map, bordered to the east by the hydro line where it left the curve of the highway, and cut straight north. Uncharted territory. She and her dad had hiked only around its edge; the rest so overgrown it wouldn't have made for easy trekking. "The Big Tangle," he had called it. There were trails in there, but their map was old and didn't show them.

"Come on, Sausage!" Kaylee called her

dog away from an intriguing snarl of brush. He hunkered down, and scooted up the daisy-lined path to join her. She smiled, her heart warming. He was such a good boy. Her partner.

Her mom said Sausage made the cabin seem more like a home. At first this had been their Canada Cottage, somewhere to stay while Mom and Dad flew water bombers. Every September, when most kids were heading back to school, she and her parents would fly back to St. Lucia. Instead of attending a regular school, she would do her lessons stretched out on white sand under a breadfruit tree, breathing deeply the musty, sweet aroma of fruit mixed with sea salt. Homeschooling they called it, though "home" was pretty mobile. When they weren't traveling, home on the island was one of the beach resort cabins her Nana and Papa now owned just north of the capital city of Castries.

But that was before. Now Canada Cottage

had become their year-round home in Booker Bay, and she hiked with Sausage instead of her dad. Instead of homeschooling, she went to class in town just like all the other kids — all because her mom decided she wanted to go to the community college. School for Mom meant no time to homeschool Kaylee, and no time to fly south to St. Lucia … and Dad.

Kaylee's breath caught as she thought of it. Her head buzzed. She wanted to scream or start running and never stop. Instead, spotting a mushroom peeking from between strawberry plants, she kicked its head off.

The last time they left St. Lucia, her mom had promised they would be back soon. But Mom had broken her promise. Kaylee had shouted angrily, and cried herself empty. She pleaded with her mom, trying to make her understand that they had to go back, that Dad might be waiting for them. Mom had cried too. She told her he wasn't waiting, and that they needed to try to rebuild their lives.

Mom was hurting. Kaylee understood that, but also knew her mom was wrong about Dad. Mom just needed time to heal, then she would want to go back. When that time came, Kaylee would be ready to fly.

Booker Bay was a good place to feel better. During the day only an occasional buzz saw or speedboat broke the quiet. At night before dropping off to sleep, Kaylee would lie in bed with her window open listening to almost nothing at all, just the sound of trees folding their leaves, and the occasional snap of twigs as some animal prowled the night.

Besides a tourist lodge, there were twelve other homes along the bay — some were lived in all year round, and others only during summer vacations. Misto, the town proper, was a good-sized community nestled on the west side of the lake with the same name. Everyone said the name came from the Cree word *mista* which means *big* but that the mapmakers got it mixed up in Ottawa. Everyone said they weren't surprised.

Big lake, big woods — Dad's "Big Tangle." The forest went on for miles, which was why the province kept a forest fire operations center there. Airplanes were always coming and going. Tourists came and went too, hundreds in the summer for the great fishing, most of them gone by September. People came for all kinds of reasons and stayed for all kinds of others.

Kaylee watched Sausage as he dashed after a gray squirrel. He zigzagged down the path in hot pursuit, smashing into the base of a poplar as his quarry vanished into the leafy top. He thrust his nose deep into the shrubs and grass at its base, snuffling all around, sneezing indignantly. After a moment he forgot the squirrel, planted his legs and began tugging at something in the underbrush.

"What have you got now, you silly thing?"

While the squirrel chattered and scolded from above, Sausage gruffed and growled, pulling in short bursts. He was getting big — big for a basset hound, anyway. Extra long legs on a breed that usually belly-scraped the ground meant he could keep up on Kaylee's daily hikes. He had been a gift from Mom last fall.

"If you're hiking all day," she had said, "I think you should have some company." Hiking was something Mom never had time for herself.

Sausage was a tiny thing then, a playful, licking bundle of fun tripping over long ears, and running nose first into the world. In the beginning, Kaylee had wanted nothing to do with him. Her dad had always been her hiking partner. No dog was going to take his place. She had shouted at her mother, accusing her of using the dog as a bribe to try to make her forget about going back to the island.

Her mom didn't say anything, but the pain in her eyes shamed Kaylee. Her mom had just wanted to make her happy. She said she was worried about Kaylee spending so much time alone.

Starting regular school for the first time in grade five had been tough. Being forced into a crowded classroom was confusing. Besides, everybody was already best friends with somebody else. Kaylee was often on her own at recess. She lived for the afternoon buzzer sounding, and the school bus rescue, delivering her back home ... where the bribe-dog waited. He would jump all over her, eagerly washing her ears and face with his tongue, and snuffling her shoes as if trying to figure out where she'd been.

After a while, she began looking forward not just to going home, but to going home to Sausage.

In the months that followed school

got easier to take, and by the end of the year she had one or two friends. Now that summer holidays were here, though, she hardly ever saw them. Other kids were fine for school, but she would only share the woods with Sausage. And her dad.

Sausage growled playfully as Kaylee got down on her hands and knees beside him, and reached into the brush beside the path. She set her jaw, and grasped the bristly stems of wild raspberry, untangling what she could. With a grunt, Sausage tumbled backward into the path, teeth clamped on the handle of what turned out to be a large axe.

"Let go, Sausage." Kaylee gently pried his jaws apart and stood the axe on end. "You see, boy?" she said. "The woods are full of surprises!" She laughed, pulled a biscuit from her pocket, and flipped it toward her dog. With a mighty *snap* Sausage caught it in the air, and swallowed it in one gulp.

"You should chew, you know!" She laughed as Sausage started his up-down-bowing-bum-in-the-air dance — his way of telling her that he wanted another biscuit. She tossed one down the path, and Sausage scurried after it.

Deep in the woods a blue jay squawked. In the distance, a floatplane powered up to take off. Somewhere, someone was barbecuing steaks. Summers around here were as close as you could get to heaven. She swallowed suddenly, her eyes brimming as she remembered that terrible morning just over a year ago.

It had been early, a gentle rain tapping at the roof of their small beach house. Her mother had walked into her room and sat down on the edge of her bed without saying a word. She stroked Kaylee's cheek, and started twisting her wedding band. She did that sometimes when she was upset.

Alarmed, Kaylee had pulled herself upright in bed. "What's wrong, Mom?"

she asked. Her mother opened her mouth to speak, then pressed Kaylee's face tight against her chest, crushing her as she began to sob.

Kaylee knew. She didn't want to know, but she did. She held her mother tight, and they rocked back and forth, crying.

Her father had been called out late the night before to do a Medevac flight. He never came back.

Chapter Three

"Do you *have* to fly today, Mom?" Kaylee hadn't touched her eggs. She turned the fork over and over on the table beside her plate.

Mom paused mid-mouthful and glanced up at her, eyebrow raised. They had this conversation almost every morning.

"We could go to the beach or something."

Her mother sighed and pushed her plate away. "Kaylee, you know I have to fly."

"Why? There's no fire around here. Why can't you just take a day off?"

"I can't do that." Her mother reached over and tilted Kaylee's chin, looking her straight in the eye. "You and I both know what's at the bottom of this, Kaylee. You're just going to have to think your way past it."

Kaylee pulled her head away and picked up a spoon, studying her reflection. Upside down eyes — green. Upside down nose — gross. "No, it's not that, Mom." She didn't sound very convincing, even to herself. After all, Dad had disappeared when he was flying.

"Kaylee," her mother said gently. "I'm a good pilot ..."

Kaylee looked up sharply. "Are you saying Dad WASN'T a good pilot?"

"No, that's not what ..."

"Well, what are you saying, then?" Kaylee's voice was getting louder; she couldn't help it. As she stood, her chair fell back onto the ceramic floor.

"Kaylee Marie, stop this." Her mother

held her shoulder firmly. "Sit with me."

After a moment, Kaylee relented. They moved to the living room sofa, and she curled into the crook of her mother's arm, listening to her heartbeat. *Thump. Thump. Thump.*

"Kaylee, we can't know what's going to happen in life. Your father was a good man. The best. And when he died ..."

"No! He DIDN'T die!" she protested, suddenly tearful, pulling away from her mother's arms. "They didn't find him. Maybe he's not dead!"

"Kaylee, we've been through this."

"Maybe he bumped his head and lost his memory. Why won't you go back and look for him?" She stood, arms straight at her sides, hands curled into fists.

"We can't change what happened ..."

"You don't know what happened. And you don't care!" Kaylee was crying now. "You just gave up. I wanted to go back, but you didn't even want to try!" She ran from the house, slamming the back door behind her, and stumbled toward the lake.

At the end of the dock, she sat sniffling, and stared into the murky water, wiping away tears. She took off her shoes and socks, and wiggled her toes in the rippling wetness, listening to the creak of the dock and the gentle bobbing of her mother's floatplane. The pontoons slapped time to the beating of her heart.

After a while, her mother's step sounded on the dock. Kaylee stared straight ahead as her mom eased herself down beside her.

A squirrel scolded them from the roof of the shed. Her mother's arm circled her shoulders. Kaylee let out a breath.

"I'm sorry, Mom."

"I'm sorry too," her mother whispered. "Things happen, sweetheart. Things that we don't expect. But we've got to find a way to keep going." She took Kaylee's hand in hers, gently prying apart her fingers.

"Sometimes we hike ... and sometimes we work." She sighed. "Remember that when your dad disappeared, he was helping someone. We can be proud of him."

The ache in Kaylee's chest was so big that she thought it might split apart. "I am proud of him, Mom." She swallowed hard. "But I don't understand why you have to keep flying."

"Because it's what I do, honey. I need to help someone too. Look, I'm a good pilot, and the radio guys at the base always know where I am. Nothing is going to happen to me." She squeezed Kaylee's hand as she said this, as if she could make her believe. "If you're ever really worried, you can tune up the King radio in the shed and listen in. Okay? You know the frequency. And if you need anything at all, Jack's right next door. Mrs. Morrison too."

Jack and Mrs. Morrison were as close to family as they had so far away from St. Lucia.

"I know, Mom." Kaylee pulled her mother's arm around her shoulders again, and leaned close. She still felt bad about yelling, but overall she felt better. A little.

Chapter Four

When Kaylee stopped by, Jack was chopping firewood, a line of sweat down his back staining his T-shirt a deeper shade of red.

"Did you lose an axe, Jack?" she asked.

Jack stopped swinging, lifted his baseball cap, and wiped his brow. "Sure is hot today, isn't it Kayls? Nope, my one and only axe is right here. Why?"

"Oh, Sausage and I found this one in the woods yesterday." Kaylee stood it on end, pivoting the blade in the dirt.

"Hah!" Jack snorted. "That dog has some nose. Or maybe it's luck. You never know what he's going to find next."

"As long as he doesn't have to go through water to get it. Sausage hates getting his feet wet."

"Ever try coaxing him with a hamburger? If there was a sunken treasure chest filled with dinner hiding in that bay, you'd see the world's first scuba-diving basset hound." Jack chuckled as he went back to his chopping. Kaylee sat down to watch.

As Jack swung the weight of his great axe back, up, and into the log, black-flies buzzed about Kaylee's neck, trying to crawl into her ears. She waved them away. The day was going to be a scorcher, the rays from the morning sun already tightening the skin on her cheeks and forehead.

She waited for Jack to put down his axe and start talking, making a silent bet as to whether they would talk about flying or how she and her mom were doing. Jack had always been a good friend, and since they came back from St. Lucia he checked in often to see if there was anything they needed. He was also a flying nut. Her whole life, she had been surrounded by flying nuts.

"Not working today, Jack?" Kaylee asked.

Jack grinned, but kept swinging. "What, you don't call this work?"

"You know what I mean. This is fire season. Shouldn't you be flying your helicopter?"

Jack propped his axe against the chopping block, stacked his firewood in a dusty green wheelbarrow, and sat on a gnarled tree stump next to Kaylee.

"I work by contract. The province doesn't hire me unless there's already a fire somewhere. Besides, my bird's in the shop right now." He sighed. "Bit of an overhaul — too much time in the air." He searched the sky. "Is your mom flying today?"

"Yeah," she said, trying to hide a smile. "Jealous?"

Jack raised his eyebrows, and looked about to protest.

"You-hoo! Mr. Mack!" Jack and Kaylee turned to see Mrs. Morrison walking up the drive in her standard fuzzy pink slippers, her snow-white hair rolled tight in curlers.

Mrs. Morrison had lived and breathed theatre her whole life. As a girl in England, she hung out backstage sewing buttons on costumes while her mom and dad rehearsed their lines. When she grew up, she studied drama in university ... then fell in love with a biologist, married him, and moved to Misto. While her husband was alive, she taught at the local high school, but now spent her days adding a touch of drama to Booker Bay.

Kaylee had always thought her fearless, or maybe a bit crazy — especially when she was zipping down the lane on her yellow motor scooter, Spot's cat-cage latched to the luggage rack. Mrs. Morrison did as she liked, dressed how she pleased, and didn't give a flip about what anyone thought. Today she complimented her slippers with bright orange knee-pants, and a red halter-top.

"Hello, Mrs. Morrison." Jack straightened to greet his elder neighbor.

"Hello back, Mr. Black-Jack," she said in her high, musical voice. "Have you seen my Spot?" She adjusted the wire-rim glasses on her nose, and peered at Kaylee.

"That dog of yours hasn't been chasing him, has he?"

"Oh-no, Mrs. Morrison," Kaylee said quickly, "You know Sausage doesn't care about anything except following his nose."

Mrs. Morrison furrowed her brow, and stuck out her bottom lip as if processing this idea. "Is that your axe, Kaylee?"

"No, Mrs. Morrison. Sausage found it in the woods. I thought maybe it was Jack's."

"It's sure not mine," Jack said. "Are you missing an axe, Mrs. Morrison?"

"No, no ... but it just so happens that I could use a new one."

Kaylee smiled. "Here — why don't you keep it Mrs. Morrison? At least till we find out where it belongs."

Mrs. Morrison pooched out her bottom lip again, head tilted to one side. "Well, yes, that's a good idea. I will keep it for now — until we find its home." Mrs. Morrison accepted the axe from Kaylee. "Now, I must find Spot!"

Jack rubbed the back of his neck. "I saw Spot in my wood pile earlier, Mrs. Morrison. I'm sure he's around here somewhere. Here, let me bring that axe over for you."

"Thank you, Mr. Wood-Stack," she trilled, relinquishing the heavy axe. Turning, she padded back down the sandy driveway, singing something about feeling pretty. Mid-lyric she paused, calling over her shoulder, "And if you see Spot again, tell him Mommy's looking for him!"

Jack and Kaylee waited until they heard the slap of her back door before they dared look at each other. As soon as they did, Kaylee burst into giggles, and Jack guffawed, smacking his knee.

"What's with the name-game, Jack?" Kaylee gasped, swallowing her laughter. "Do you think she's losing her marbles?"

"Oh, no, Kaylee," Jack said with a grin. "Mrs. Morrison's all right — quick as a beetle I'd say, and made of pretty tough mettle. She's just having fun. She does love that cat, though."

"Her cat named Spot," Kaylee said, chortling.

"Hey," Jack said, pretending to be stern. "That's no more unusual than a dog named Sausage!"

"I suppose." Kaylee grinned. She slapped at a blackfly. "I wish we had some wind to blow these little creeps out of here!"

"Yeah, it's getting pretty muggy. Wouldn't be surprised to see a storm later."

"Then I'm going hiking right now!" She tossed a mock salute her neighbor's way and started off. "See you later, Jack."

"Bye, Kayls," Jack said.

Chapter Five

Black poplar tops branched over the path, joining with birch and jack pine, offering some shelter from the brutal sun. As always, Kaylee's senses sharpened while she walked. Through the soles of her scuffed sneakers she could feel every twist and uneven step along the path. In the distance she could make out the grumble of a generator starting up. Closer in and all around, sparrows twittered and ravens croaked and pinged at play. The woods were hot and dry. She could smell the dust and must of old dead leaves. The tap of her faithful walking stick kept time with her own thumping heart as she lengthened her stride, keeping up with her dog.

Kaylee brought her walking stick along on every hike. She had found it during a trek with her dad. He thought the top looked like the head of a loon and had laughed, saying she would be loony to walk without a stick. She smiled. Walking in the woods reminded her of so many happy times with her dad.

At a cluster of fireweed and poison ivy she paused. Was that an opening? It was a path, she was sure of it, leading deep into Green Sector. Stepping into the fireweed as far as she could, she used her walking stick to shove the poison ivy to the side. She knew it! She knew there were paths in there!

The story went that a long time ago mushroom pickers had created a whole network of paths in these woods. Kids at school told tales of poachers, murderers, and other bad people who used the trails after the mushroom pickers were gone, but she didn't believe them.

Should she follow it? She wanted to, but what if there really were bad people in the woods? Sometimes she heard sounds, chopping sounds and an occasional shout, and couldn't tell where they were coming from. Maybe she should wait, and come back with her mom or Jack.

Growff! Sausage leaped past Kaylee into the new opening, making her jump.

"Sausage!" she called. He ignored her and plunged nose down into the brush at a twist in the vague path. He must have spotted another squirrel.

"Sausage, come back!" Nothing. Oh well. Might as well wait here, she thought. He'll be back just as soon as the squirrel runs up a tree.

Yaaarpp!

So much for waiting. She had never heard Sausage yelp like that. Hacking the ivy away from the opening, she sprinted down the path to where her dog had disappeared.

Yaarpp-yaarpp-yaarpp!

Frantically, she pushed her way into the brush. She found Sausage in a small clearing beside a fallen log. He was thrashing about on his side, one leg raised awkwardly and caught fast. His leg was caught in a trap, and he was struggling to pull it out.

His crying was hoarse from panic.

"Sausage! Easy boy ... easy." She wrapped her arms around him, trying to hold him still. He twisted and pulled. She hugged him tighter, until he started to calm.

Yaaaowww! Yaaaoooww!

His cries wrenched at her heart, but she needed him to be still in order to examine the trap. "Easy boy ... " she soothed, her own heart racing. The trap was dirty metal — the leg-hold kind. It was clamped just above his back right paw.

She held him tight, laying her weight

across him in an effort to keep him steady while she studied the trap. Who would leave such a thing here? She reached for her walking stick and tried to pry the trap jaws apart with its pointed tip. It didn't budge — the spring was too strong.

Sausage lay still now, shivering. His heart rat-tat-tatted against the barrel of his chest.

"Poor Sausage, poor baby. It's okay ..." Kaylee's voice caught in her throat. What was she going to do? She didn't want to leave him to get help. She had heard stories about animals biting their feet off in order to get free from traps like this. She studied it again, brushing away dirt and pulling dried grass from its hinges. There had to be a release on here somewhere!

Yes. She felt matching levers on either side of the jaws. She squeezed one between her fingers and the heel of her hand. It gave a little, but just on the one side.

"Be a good boy, Sausage. Lie still." Keeping her weight on top of the dog, she took her other arm from around his neck. He shifted, but she pushed her weight into him, forcing him still. "Good boy ... good boy," she crooned.

He shuddered underneath her, but didn't move. She reached down and put one hand on either side of the trap jaws, squeezing both levers at the same time. They were stiff, but they did give a little.

"Come on Kaylee ... " she grunted, her body lifting a little in her effort.

The trap gave way just as Sausage leapt from underneath her.

YOWP! He jerked out from the trap, twisting awkwardly. He was free!

Hurt paw raised, Sausage limped back and forth in a small half circle. *Arp, arp, arp,* he cried, seeming unsure of whether to sit or walk.

Kaylee crouched beside him, burying her head in the ruff of his neck.

He accepted her touch and twitched his tail back and forth, trying to lay his head in her lap.

"Oh Sausage ... poor boy ..." She probed his sore leg softly with her fingertips. The skin wasn't broken ... there had been rubber lining the jaws of the trap. Still, something might be broken inside.

Sausage's whimpering had calmed to a distressed, whistling kind of breathing. He was able to set his leg back down so that his paw just touched the ground. She had to get him to the vet.

"Come on, Sausage. Can you walk, boy?" She picked up her walking stick and used it to push aside brush until they were back on the path. Walking slowly, she encouraged the dog to limp alongside her, stopping often to rub him about the ears.

Thankfully, Jack was home, and drove them immediately to the animal clinic.

In the examination room, Jack grasped Sausage around his barrel chest and hind-quarters, and lifted him gently to the table. Kaylee cradled her pet's head, stroking his neck, scratching under his collar, as the vet examined his injury.

"Is he going to be okay Dr. Roberts?"

The veterinarian straightened, nodding her head. "He's going to be fine, Kaylee, thanks to your quick rescue," she said warmly. "He's twisted his leg, and there will probably be some swelling from broken blood vessels, but it could have been much worse. Leg-hold traps can cause extensive damage to the blood supply. If Sausage had been caught for any amount of time, we might have had to amputate."

Kaylee gulped, gently stroking Sausage between the ears. "I guess we were lucky."

"I'll give him a sedative for now. Massage his leg as gently as you can over the next day or two, and wrap it with a hot cloth to take care of any swelling. Just make sure he takes it easy for a while."

"Thanks, Dr. Roberts," Kaylee said, relieved.

Jack carried Sausage back to the truck, set him on the seat between them, and started the engine. He looked grim most of the way back to Booker Bay, muttering under his breath and shaking his head. "I can't believe someone set a trap in there, so close to where folks are living."

"Are there poachers in the woods around here, Jack?"

"Haven't heard anything like that, but I suppose anything is possible." Jack glanced down at Sausage, curled awkwardly on the seat, sedated, his head bouncing from its resting place with every pothole they passed over. "Lucky that trap didn't break any bones."

Sausage thumped his tail as Kaylee stroked his head.

"Yeah," she said. "In a few days he'll be right as rain."

Chapter Six

Crack!

Kaylee sat up straight in her bed, torn from her dream by a reverberating crash. It still pinged in her mind, tingled her fingertips. She wiped the sleep from her eyes, listening to rolling thunder. Rain tattooed the roof and windows like thousands of running feet, and wind slapped and scratched tree branches against the side of their house.

She walked to the window and peeked past the curtains. What a show! Lightning forked across the sky into the forest all around. Sheet lightning torched the cloud cover, and kept the sky bright. A rumble instantly followed another flash, swelling, growing, and rolling — then gone. Kaylee closed her eyes and imagined standing below a trellis with a freight train passing overhead. The storm was full upon them.

When she was little, Kaylee would sit close beside her dad and watch thunderstorms, shivering as the air chilled, and jumping with every crack as the sky ripped itself apart. Not Dad, though. He loved storms, and would treat every light show like fireworks. "It's like Carnival back home! Did you see that one, my girl?" he would ask, grinning, his eyes flashing like the lightning.

One afternoon they took shelter in the front porch from a storm that had brewed big, black, and loud. Her dad laughed each time she jumped at a boom of thunder. When it started to hail, he grabbed an empty ice cream bucket, and two tin mixing bowls from the pantry. "Come on, Kaylee!" he called, grinning. He popped one bowl on her head, and one on his own. "Hard hats," he said, and pulled her out with him to their winter-washed yard. They giggled and slipped, trying to out-shout the pinging on their metal hats, and keep their balance, while scooping the ice-balls into their bucket.

He never let her hide when she was frightened. He would bring her right into the spinning, laughing, topsy-turvy middle of things, but as long as she was with him she knew everything would work out okay.

Tears spilled from her eyes and streamed hot and wet, along the curve of her cheeks. She pressed her face against the cool window. Some day her dad would come back to them. He would. He could have lost his memory when he crashed — that happened to people all the time. He could have ended up on any one of the dozens of small islands near where they lived. Some day he would remember. Some day he would come back.

He would have liked this storm. It was big. Kaylee wiped her face and looked around the yard. The trees were swaying, but upright. The crash that woke her must have been a lightning strike. It must have been close.

She sat back down on her bed, weary. At least tomorrow, she would have a day with her mom.

Chapter Seven

"Okay. Thanks, Bob."

Mom hung up the phone and turned to Kaylee. "A fire's sprung up a few hours west. They're calling for ground crews, and two of our bombers are on their way. Could be a big one. I've got to get to the center. They've got me on stand-by in case they need me."

"What?" Kaylee looked up from the table, stung. "You said you'd go hiking with me today. It's your day off!"

"I know, hon. I'm sorry." Mom touched Kaylee's cheek. "It can't be helped. It's a bad time of year — everything is so dry."

Kaylee jerked away from her mother's touch, pouting into her toast. It was always the same.

"You always have to work on the nice days," she said.

"I know, Kaylee. If we had a good long rain, they probably wouldn't need me. Maybe next time we should plan for fun on a rainy day, hey?" She ruffled Kaylee's hair, trying to cheer her up.

"It rained last night. Didn't that help?"

"Yes, it rained, but it was the wrong kind of rain. The ground is so hard the water doesn't have a chance to soak in before it evaporates, and it's so dry that lightning is triggering new fires all over the north."

"You promised."

"I'm sorry."

Those words were like a wet Band-Aid. They just didn't stick.

"You're always, sorry," Kaylee snapped. "And you're always breaking promises!"

"Kaylee ... don't be like this."

"Don't be like what?" She stood, glaring at her mother now. "Always waiting for you to change your mind? To break your promises? You promised to spend time with me today, just like you promised we'd go back to St. Lucia!"

"Kaylee!" Her mother stepped back as if she'd been slapped.

"You don't care about me!" Kaylee wailed. "Just like you don't care about Dad — or Nana and Papa!"

"I do care, Kaylee! You know I do."

Kaylee couldn't listen to any more. "Just go to work, then. Fine!" she shouted. "That's all you ever do." She ran to her room, slamming the door behind her, and flung herself on her bed, the blood pounding in her ears. After a while she calmed, and listened for her mother's knock. It didn't come. All she heard was the ticking of the clock hanging in the living room.

"I have to go now, Kaylee." Her mother's

voice outside her door. Kaylee didn't answer.

"I love you, honey. I'll be back as soon as I can."

Keys scraped as her mother gathered her things from the counter, and the door slapped shut behind her. A few minutes later, the truck rumbled into gear.

Kaylee sat up, punched her pillow, and wandered to the back deck. At least Sausage wouldn't let her down. He was snoozing in the sun, but rolled over for a belly scratch when she sat down beside him.

Spying his empty food dish, Kaylee smiled. Sausage loved food more than anything — even walks with Kaylee, but after his injury he had refused to eat. Now, after a few days rest, and plenty of hot leg wraps, the swelling was gone. He was eating, and walking with a slight limp.

Kaylee lay back on the wooden planks already warmed by the sun. Another scorcher. What else was new? With a sigh, she rose to her feet. "With or without Mom," she said to her dog, "I'm going for a hike."

Sausage sat up straight, thumping his tail eagerly on the deck, watching her.

"Sorry, Sausage," Kaylee said. "You've got to stay home for a few more days."

She made a kissing sound, calling him into the house. After pinning her feather on the map — Red Sector — she grabbed her walking stick and left, shutting Sausage inside. "You stay in," she said through the window. "You can't follow me today."

Sausage's whine followed her as she walked away.

She hadn't gone far down her favorite sandy path when she heard, and felt, the deep drone of a water bomber. Its engine vibrated in her teeth. She stopped, craning her neck, watching until she saw the brief flash of yellow through the treetops. It was low. Just taking off, she supposed. Could that have been Mom's way of telling her she had to go to the big fire? She hadn't seen enough of the plane to tell if it had her mother's number thirty-seven on it.

So what, she thought. Flying or sitting at the airport on standby, Mom had still broken her promise.

Even under the forest canopy, sweat trickled down the back of her neck. It was hot like a sauna — dry heat, not quite enough to burn the insides of her nose when she breathed in, but almost.

Kaylee came to the path she had happened on the other day, the one leading into Green Sector. Her mom had told her to stay away from it until she could check it out, worried there might be more hidden traps.

Somewhere in the back of her brain, she registered the sound of another aircraft taking off. She liked living near the airport, enjoying the rumble of engines, the sight of aircraft slicing through the air, circling the landing strip and each other. She liked the planes; she just had trouble getting into one.

She took a few steps down the forbidden path. If her mom had kept her promise, they would be exploring Green Sector together. It wasn't Kaylee's fault her mom would rather work.

She would just go a little way, she decided. The forest pressed close as she stepped lightly over clumps of Labrador tea and juniper shrubs. She poked her walking stick in tangled areas — just in case.

In spite of the undergrowth, she could tell that this had been a well-used path at one time. A bunch of years ago, a fire had burned up the shrubs and some of the trees in this part of the woods. Pine trees, and others with tough bark had survived. The next year, morel mushrooms appeared — a gourmet treat prized by chefs around the world. They always grew like crazy one year after a fire, and then they were gone.

A lady from Vancouver had flown in and spoken at a town meeting, saying she would pay lots of money for the things. That had set off a rush. Mushroom pickers flooded the area like old-time prospectors hurrying to stake claims for gold, tramping out crisscrossing paths, searching every possible nook and ditch for their treasure.

Not anymore, though. No more mushrooms, no more pickers. This path was partly grown in, but she could still follow it. Who might have used it after the mushroom pickers were gone? Remembering the leg-trap, she thought briefly about the unsettling stories she had heard at school.

A helicopter beat the air close by. Busy day at the airport!

In the deep calm of the woods, Kaylee felt sorry she had gotten angry earlier and was glad that if her mom had to fly anywhere, it was to that fire out west.

She didn't like her flying where there were too many other airplanes around. Her mom was a good pilot, but who knew how good the other guys were?

Her foot caught under the trunk of a twisted jack pine lying across her path. Great, she thought, too tangled to move out of the way. She'd have to climb over it. A water bomber rumbled nearby. That was odd. They should all be out at that big fire. She couldn't see much through the treetops, but by the sound of things the bomber was somewhere in the direction of town. She looked again to the forest roof as poplar branches rustled and swayed a little. The wind had picked up.

"Yeeouch!" Her focus jerked back to ground level. With her nose to the treetops she hadn't noticed the broken end of a prickly branch until she had scratched the length of her forearm. She licked at the deepest part of the scratch — salty from sweat and blood that had risen to the surface. An angry white line swelled, surrounded by pink. Served her right for not looking.

Scrambling over the rest of the tree, she worked her way on up the path. It seemed to be going uphill. Good. A high spot would give her a better view of what was going on with those airplanes.

The underbrush thinned and gave way to a rocky slope. Turning her feet to the side, she climbed, gripping outcrops, her stick dug firmly into depressions, trying not to slip on loose stones. Finally, she was at the top of the hill. Compared to the path she had just come from this was a wide-open space — just a few trees whipped by the wind. That had sure come up suddenly!

Then she looked to the edge of the clearing and her jaw dropped.

Billowing white and black smoke filled the sky to the west. A huge cloud ate up the sky. In the distance, a mustard yellow water bomber glinted, dwarfed against the massive smoke cloud. Another plane circled from the other side, and a tiny dot of a helicopter slung a bucket from the lake.

"A forest fire?" she choked. "Here?"

Her mother would be trying to reach her. She had to get home.

Taking off at a gallop, Kaylee skidded down the rocky slope on her backside, and barreled a fair way down the path before realizing she had dropped her walking stick.

It would have to wait — she had to get home fast! The path closed in on her. "Ow!" she gasped, as a thin sapling whipped across her cheek. Pressing her palm against the sting, she bounded around the next corner.

Here the path was less clogged, and she was able to pick up her pace even more. Her side ached, but she had to keep going. As she filled her lungs with great gulps of air, she could smell just a hint of wood smoke.

She raced through a small patch of fireweed, then stopped short in the middle of the bright pink blossoms. These hadn't been on the path when she climbed the hill.

Where was she?

Chapter Eight

Kaylee spun around, pushing her way back through shoulder-high fireweed the way she had come. She paused at the edge of the bush, gasping, her chest heaving and stared at the outlines of what had once been two separate paths. Both were almost closed in with foxtail. She had no idea from which she had just come. Turning, she checked the sky over the clearing. The smoke cloud was still there, but not as big as before, she thought. Or was it? A breeze bent the fireweed, bringing another whiff of smoke. It smelled like camping.

One of the paths was a little less clogged with underbrush and had a wild rose bush to the side. Had she seen that before? Betting that she had, she plunged back into the forest.

The forest ceiling was too tangled to see much of what was happening above, but the drone of water bombers was constant. *Thwap-thwap* went a chopper, maybe two, in the distance.

"Oomph!" Her right foot twisted under a raised poplar root, and she landed flat-out on the path.

Winded, she pressed her right cheek into the dirt, heart pounding, mind racing. As her lungs filled with air, and her pulse slowed, a new thought scratched through. The fire-fighting base for their entire region was right here in Misto. She had been hearing aircraft for a while ... maybe the fire was almost out.

Spitting out sand and pine needles, she climbed to her feet, gingerly testing her ankle. Twisted. Too bad she had dropped her walking stick. She thought of her dad, a painful lump forming in her throat. What would he do?

He would go back and pick up the walking stick.

"Come on, Kaylee," she muttered. "You're loony to walk without a stick!" His words gave her a small burst of comfort. She would go on. Her ankle was only twisted. She could walk it out.

Okay, she had taken a wrong turn somewhere. She needed to calm down and figure things out. The fire was under control — of course it was! Running was silly, dangerous even. She knew these woods like the back of her hand. Well, most of the woods, anyway. Those dumb old mushroom pickers had left way too many paths.

Spotting a crushed pop can jammed against a gnarl of a black spruce, she stopped. Who had been using these woods lately?

She pressed her hand against the scaly, gray bark beside the can, deciding not to move it. It would make a good marker. Why hadn't she seen it earlier? Running too fast, she supposed. Her cheek where she had been slapped by the sapling felt bruised.

I'll walk a little farther, she thought. If it's not the right way I can always turn back.

Was her mom fighting this fire or had she gone to the other one out west? Probably this one. If her mom had gone west, she would have been called back. She would be worried about her daughter. She had probably asked Jack to check on her.

Kaylee stopped.

Hug a tree. That's what the kids in school were taught to do if they got lost, hug a tree until they were found. Jack would know she was in the woods. After all, she went hiking pretty much every day. He would come looking for her. He kept a key to their house, just in case. He would let himself in and check the map for her feather.

She needed to do what she had been taught. Wait.

But she had pinned the feather on Red Sector.

Something snapped in the woods to her left. Just a fox, most likely. In town, old Mr. Frank always had pelts hanging behind the trading counter of his general store. Mostly fox, but sometimes he had lynx and would let her stroke the pelt. It was the softest thing she had ever felt, softer than a baby's hair. Lynx were rare, hard to trap, and mean when cornered.

A poacher would be mean too.

It was probably just a fox.

All she could see of the sky were scattered puzzle-pieces of light. The bombers sounded louder now. She swallowed. The inside of her mouth had a flat, rusty sort of taste, and her eyes stung a little. She stared hard into the brush around her. It didn't look smoky. Still ... what if the fire wasn't almost out? Needing more air she opened her mouth, sucking deeper. What if Jack couldn't find her?

Another blackfly bit. She slapped her neck, hard.

No. She was not going to just stand there making like lunch for blackflies and fresh bait for poachers, waiting for the forest to burn down around her!

Stepping lightly, she started a slow jog along the path, keeping the weight off her injured ankle. Once she got back to her hill she would see what was happening. If the fire was almost out, *then* she would hug a tree and wait for Jack to find her. That was pretty close to home, and if he was calling her she could shout back.

Really, she thought, she didn't even need Jack. She had taken a dumb turn before because she wasn't thinking straight. She wouldn't make that mistake twice.

The pain in her ankle had almost worked itself out, and she quickened her pace. Around a twist in the path, she stopped to push aside a few willow shoots and stepped into a small clearing. Poplar branches had woven themselves into a leafy roof, making a green cave. A few stumps in the center surrounded what was left of a small circle of stones. She coughed, the air heavy with old dust. The stones had been kicked around a bit and, inside what must have been a fire pit, runners of Creeping Charlie wound around each other, over and under, tiny purple flowers peeking from heart-shaped leaves.

She had never been in this clearing before.

"This is not good," she said, her voice hoarse, her throat dry and scratchy.

Better backtrack to where she had found the fireweed. As she retraced her path, she listened carefully to the distant vibration of aircraft. Once in a while, a gust of wind above the treetops would bring the engine noise much closer. She watched her feet, placing one sneaker in front of the other, bouncing her worries backward and forward, hoping the fire was almost out, anxious that it might not be.

When she got to the old pop can, she paused again. She hadn't noticed before, but another path led from this spot — one that looked like it went slightly up hill.

"Yes!" she cried, relief washing over her. This had to be the right path!

Watching for stray roots, she jogged up the trail. She would be back on her hill in no time. Better hurry. Mom would be worried, and Jack would be searching for her.

Around a corner she came to another fork. One path disappeared into the tangled brush to her right, and another one continued up the slope.

"Just keep climbing, Kaylee," she breathed. The opening of the new path was plush with moss and gated with ferns. As she barreled her way past, she chided herself for running helter-skelter through the woods. That was a number one way to get lost!

A grade niner had gone missing in the woods a few years back. She didn't know him but heard that he used to go hunting all the time. One day he was out with his dad and cousins pushing bush, trying to drive out deer, only he didn't come out where he was supposed to. They never found him. He must have panicked, she thought.

The RCMP started their "Hug a Tree" program right after that.

Kaylee came to another off-shoot in the path — one with a fallen over jack pine not too far ahead.

"Almost there," she puffed and began running the mostly clay offshoot. Where

the path was blocked she stopped and climbed carefully over the prickly branches of the dead tree. Her shirt was sticky with sweat, and blackflies buzzed around her neck.

On the other side she stopped, confused. The path ended at a wide, open area. This wasn't her hill, she realized with growing dread. She walked into the clearing, eyes glued to the sky, mouth sour. The smoke cloud looked twice as big as before and was mostly brown and black. She thought she could see orange in it too. It was close.

The wind whipped around the clearing, bending treetops at its edge. Ashes fluttered past, some sticking to the damp of her shirt.

"Wildfire!"

Chapter Nine

"Come on, Kaylee," she breathed. "The fire just looks bigger because of the wind."

In her heart she knew that wasn't true, but saying it made her feel better. She scanned the clearing more closely, this time spotting the power cable. It wasn't a clearing at all — it was the hydro line! Cables ran as far as she could see from one side of her to the other, strung from pole to pole. The grass had been shaved short underneath and for several feet on either side.

Tears of relief sprang to her eyes. The power line ran north-south along the east side of Green Sector until it reached a bend in the highway close to Booker Bay. All she had to do was turn right and jog south along the line to get home. But what was waiting for her? In the distance the hydro line disappeared into a wall of smoke.

Kaylee swallowed. She had no choice. She guessed from what she had seen earlier that the fire was south — closer to Misto than Booker Bay. If she followed the hydro line toward the smoke, she would eventually reach the highway and be able to cut away home well before reaching the fire. Then she would radio her mom.

The wind was steady now, whipping her hair back from her shoulders, drying the sweat around her neck. Bracing herself, she jogged toward the smoke cloud. An occasional gust caused tree saplings to bend and bow, and threatened to throw her off-step.

The air was getting smoky. At least

three planes circled over the fire now. Two helicopters slung water buckets. She had never been so happy to see those airplanes! Her mom was surely in one of them.

How brave her mother was! Every day she was ready to fight a forest fire just like this one. Every fire, she would swoop down on a lake, swallow a bomber-bellyful of water and find the perfect place to drop it over acres of burning brush. Her mom was a good pilot. Why should Kaylee be nervous about going up in her mother's little floatplane? Flying that must be a piece of cake compared to flying a water bomber.

In spite of the haze, she could make out the aircraft better now. They were bigger. Either the fire was growing, or she was getting closer to it — and home.

Wood smoke stung her eyes. She stopped for a moment, panting, hands on her knees. Ashes sailed past. No stopping now —

home was close. Once she hit the high-way, it would be easy.

The jogging was slower now because of the smoke. She had enough scrapes and bruises for one day. The last thing she needed was to stick her foot in a gopher hole! A big black boulder stood in the clearing not too far ahead. Or maybe a bush. Odd.

The boulder moved, sort of rolled, and Kaylee froze mid-step. It was moving away from her toward the fire. A black bear!

She slipped quickly under the cover of the brush and trees to her left. It hadn't seen her. Why would a bear be heading for the fire? Then she remembered. Bears were always showing up at fires, Mom had told her, looking for the ground crew camps. Where there were fire camps, there was food, and the bears wanted it!

The bear couldn't have smelled her because she was downwind. Who could smell anything except smoke anyway? She decided to stay in the trees and follow at a safe distance. The slow pace was maddening — the bear wasn't in any great hurry. Mom must be freaking by now.

The bear stopped briefly by a break in the trees before continuing along the cut-line. An access road! Relief rippled through Kaylee as she realized the access road would cut across to where the highway looped around Booker Bay.

Tree-by-tree, Kaylee moved forward, eyes on the bear. She longed to make a mad dash for the road, but what if the bear turned and saw her? After all she had been through today, she did not think she could handle being face-to-face with a bear.

The bear ambled along the hydro line toward the fire. He didn't look back.

Finally, Kaylee neared the break in the trees. Just beyond a small raspberry patch, and through a stand of paper birch she saw the access road. She couldn't wait.

Grasping bristly shoots of raspberry to keep them from scratching her legs, she plowed through the bushes, and cut quickly through the trees. "Yes!" she cried — bear or no bear — as she left the dirt access road, and her feet hit the hot blacktop of the highway.

She took off at a sprint toward home.

A bomber came in low, just over the treetops heading toward the lake. Number thirty-seven — Mom! Sirens whined in the distance, and the air was thick with smoke and engine noise. Kaylee darted down a narrow path, a shortcut.

So close to home, she began to feel the sting of tiny scrapes all over her body and the grit of dirt ground into places it shouldn't be. A bath would feel great later. First, she had to find out from her mom exactly what was going on. The noise of engines and sirens made her nervous. The fire base for the region was based right here in Misto. How could a fire come so close?

She broke out of the woods onto the lane and stopped, stunned. Her neighbors were running from their homes, and an RCMP truck with lights flashing and siren screaming was driving slowly along the lane.

"Get out now!" someone shouted through a loud speaker. "Booker Bay is being evacuated. Leave everything! GO!"

Another officer dashed from house to house, pounding on doors.

"Kaylee!" Jack was running toward her. "Where have you been? Your mother is worried sick!"

"I know Jack ... " Kaylee broke off, choking, as Jack reached her. Suddenly, it all overwhelmed her. She grabbed hold of him, and sobbed into his shirt.

"Hey, Kaylee." Jack patted the back of her head. "Come on ... it's okay." He gripped one of her shoulders — hard — and looked her in the eyes. "We'll talk later. We have to get out of here. Now!"

Taking her hand, Jack ran with Kaylee toward his truck, opened the driver's door, boosted her in and climbed in beside her. The engine revved and he backed swiftly into the lane.

"We've got to get word to your mom. Radio dispatch called me an hour ago when the fire started to pick up. Your mom sent a message to find you and keep you close." Jack slowed briefly, as another neighbor backed into the lane. "I checked Red Sector — I looked everywhere! If you hadn't showed up when you did ..." He shook his head, and let out a deep breath.

"How did this happen, Jack?"

"Lightning, I guess," he said, frowning, eyes straight ahead. Worry lines creased his forehead as he bumped the truck along the curving lane. "The wind didn't help."

Kaylee looked to the side of the road. She thought she could see a few licks of flame in the woods, but her eyes might be playing tricks in all the smoke. How had this happened? Earlier, stretched out on the deck, she had thought it a perfect summer morning.

A chill struck her. "We've got to go back," she said, gripping Jack's arm.

He glanced toward her. "What are you talking about?"

"We've got to go back!" She was screaming now. "I've got to get Sausage!"

Chapter Ten

"Turn around, Jack!" Kaylee shouted. "Sausage is shut in the house — we've got to get him!"

Jack kept his hands firmly on the wheel, his lips drawn tightly together.

"We can't go back, Kaylee." He looked grim. "There's no time."

"We've got to!" Kaylee sobbed, pulling desperately on Jack's sleeve.

Jack's jaw was set. "We can't go back, Kaylee!" he said sharply. He pried her grip loose, and held her hand for a moment, speaking gently, "I'm sorry, Kayls."

They were almost at the highway, barely

visible for all the smoke and flying ashes. An RCMP officer waved Jack toward an area where the other residents of Booker Bay had hastily gathered.

"Jack, Sausage is my friend. He needs me," Kaylee pleaded. "I've got to go back for him!" How could she explain to Jack? She couldn't leave Sausage. He was expecting her to come back for him. She couldn't let him die.

"Kaylee, you've got to listen to me." Jack shut off the engine. "It's too dangerous for us to go back now. I know you love Sausage, and maybe he'll be fine — animals have a way of getting through things. But we have to stay out of the way of people like your mom until this fire is under control."

Kaylee dropped her head, tears running down her bare legs. How could Jack do this?

"You stay here," he said quietly. "I've got to get a message to your mom."

Jack hopped out of the cab, and made his way toward the RCMP officer.

Kaylee's eyes blurred as she glanced at her neighbors, hoping that somehow Sausage was with them. He wasn't. The Nichols twins were playing in the sand, laughing together as if nothing was wrong. Their mom, Tracy, stood nearby in her baking apron wringing her hands as she spoke with Mrs. Simpson, her next door neighbor. Jack and several others gathered around the RCMP car, watching the activity in the sky. Kaylee slipped out of the truck and looked back down the lane. The house wasn't that far. Why couldn't Jack have taken her back? It would have only taken a second.

Then she saw it — there, at the edge of the road — a bicycle! Maybe someone had ridden it out because they didn't have a car, or maybe it was here from before. It didn't matter. It was here, and Kaylee needed it.

She glanced back to where everyone was gathered. They were all looking in the direction of the fire. She dashed to where the bike was lying at the top of a sloping ditch, grabbed hold, and pulled it into the ditch with her, ducking out of sight. Checking to make sure she hadn't been noticed, she pushed the bike a little farther along. When she reached a thick patch of fireweed, she ducked into the middle of it and pushed the bike up and toward the woods. Partly hidden in brush and smoke, she cut along the edge back toward the access road.

Kaylee needn't have worried. Jack and the rest had their eyes glued to the sky.

Moments later she was bouncing back along the road toward home, the wind at her back. She gulped lungfuls of choking smoke. Her eyes burned; sirens and bomber engines roared in her ears.

Finally, she was back on her lane. She stopped briefly and looked around.

Everything looked spooky. Deserted.

Just as she was about to ride on, a noise stopped her, a noise completely at odds with the chaos of the moment.

She couldn't believe her ears. Singing? Sure enough, the tune started again, muffled, high-pitched and way off key.

"Mrs. Morrison!" Kaylee gasped. She dropped the bike, and ran up her neighbor's front walk. "Mrs. Morrison!" she called, pounding on the front door.

The singing continued.

What was going on? Kaylee tried the door. Locked. She looked up at the high shuttered windows — all closed and out of reach. Mrs. Morrison kept her windows shut tight all year round, saying the noises of the forest bothered her cat, Spot. She ran around to the back deck and peered through the kitchen window. From there she could see Mrs. Morrison stretched out on her sofa, stereo headset on, a jelly-mask draped over her eyes. She was waving

one hand in the air and singing something about a captain. Spot was standing on the back of the sofa, hair raised and teeth bared in what looked like a hiss.

"Mrs. Morrison!" Kaylee shouted again, slapping her palms against the window. Mrs. Morrison had no idea that the forest was burning down around her. She had missed the evacuation!

Kaylee tried the door ... locked. She looked around frantically, and spotted the axe she had given Mrs. Morrison. Scrambling down the steps, she grabbed it from beside the garden shed and hauled it back up with her to the kitchen door. She closed her eyes and summoned what strength she had left. With a deep breath she swung the axe up, and over her shoulder ...

Smash!!! ... through the closed window, letting it fall to the other side.

Spot yowled and spit. He leapt onto his mistress's belly, claws extended. Mrs. Morrison yelled mid-note, and sat up, tearing off her jelly-mask, and headphones. She grabbed hold of Spot and fumbled for her glasses.

"Just WHAT do you think you're doing?" she sputtered as Kaylee reached through the shattered window and let herself in. Mrs. Morrison looked around, confused. With the headphones off, she could hear the noise of the airplanes, and sirens. "What ... what?"

"You have to go, Mrs. Morrison — Booker Bay is evacuated! There's a forest fire!"

With Spot under one arm, Mrs. Morrison jumped up and ran to open the front door, fuzzy pink slippers slapping the heels of her feet. "Oh, my," she said, seeing the smoke. "Well, let's go!"

While Spot yowled and struggled to free himself, Mrs. Morrison crooked a pinkie finger and plucked her keys and a helmet from a hook. "Come on, Kaylee!" she called. "You come with us — you can sit behind me, in front of Spot's cage."

"I can't, Mrs. Morrison," Kaylee said, racing out at her heels, eyeing the hissing, spitting cat. "I've got to get Sausage — besides, I've got a ride!"

Mrs. Morrison glanced at Kaylee's bike and nodded. "Well, that's fine," she crooned, struggling to push Spot into his cage and wheel her motor scooter out from behind an overgrown lilac bush. "But we're going to wait right here for you. Do hurry along!"

Kaylee looked around. The smoke and flying ash was much heavier. Now she was positive there were flames in the woods. She left Mrs. Morrison and dashed toward her own house two doors down.

"Sausage!" she called.

Sausage barked in answer, that hoarse, hound-dog belling she loved so much. She took the steps two at a time, and flung open the front door. Sausage jumped at her, still barking, trying to lick her face.

He obviously hadn't liked being left home and was very happy to see her.

Kaylee hugged him back. "Come on Sausage ... not now. We have to go, boy!"

She turned and sprinted back down the front steps toward the lane, patting her leg, calling Sausage to come with her. She stopped at the sound of Sausage's whine. He stood at the top of the steps, tail wagging.

"Come on Sausage!" She whistled, and patted her leg again. "Come ON Sausage!" she cried. "We've got to go NOW!"

Sausage took one step forward, then backed up, whining.

Crack! Kaylee turned, startled. A tall, blazing tree had splintered across the lane. Before Kaylee could react, the flames roared across Jack's property, licking up and over the frame of his house.

She heard a scream.

"Mrs. Morrison!"

Chapter Eleven

The deafening drone of a water bomber muted the roar of the fire for a moment. Kaylee looked up as the big yellow plane came in low overhead and, with its hatches swinging open, dropped hundreds of gallons of water in front of Jack's house. The flaming tree was crushed, and the whole area was soaked. The forest beyond, however, still burned furiously. The fire had leapt the road farther on. Kaylee could not get through.

Mrs. Morrison and her motor scooter had disappeared.

As the aircraft climbed skyward and angled back toward the lake, Kaylee could

just make out the number on its nose —
thirty-seven.

"Mom!" Kaylee cried.

With Sausage at her heal, she ran into
the lane to where she had last seen her
neighbor. "Mrs. Morrison!" Where had she
gone? The forest was in flames, as was
Jack's house. She must have seen the tree
about to fall and gone for help. The scream
Kaylee heard must have been a warning.

There wasn't much time. Giving Jack's
property a wide berth, she and Sausage
circled back to her own house and around
to the work shed by the dock. The old
King radio was already tuned to the fire
frequency. As she turned it on, it let out
a sharp static burst, then a volley of crackling
transmissions.

" ... almost on the houses. Over"

"Base, this is Three-Seven. It's there
already! I made a drop, and I think I saw
Kaylee ... I'm going in again. Over."

"Three-Seven, this is Base. Check, you're going in again. Negative on Kaylee. Repeat, negative on Kaylee. She's at the highway. Over."

"Base, I saw her, and I'm going in again!"

"Check that, Three-Seven. Report off the water."

A pause in the transmissions gave Kaylee her chance. The hand-held mike was the size and shape of a computer mouse. She unhooked it from the side of the radio, pressed the "speak" lever, and held it close to her mouth.

"Mom! I'm here, Mom!" She remembered to let go of the "speak" lever when she finished talking. If she didn't, she would block the frequency and no one could get through.

"Kaylee? Kaylee is that you, honey? Are you in the shed?" Her mom sounded frantic.

"I'm okay, Mom." A lump grew in her

throat, and tears blurred her sight. "Mrs. Morrison was with me, but she's gone. I don't know if she made it out. I don't know what to do!"

"It's okay, hon. I'm off the water now, and I'm coming in for another drop. You'll be okay."

Another static burst. "Base checks you off the water, Three-Seven. Call over your target."

"Roger, Base," Mom answered, her voice tight and controlled.

"Kaylee, this is Base. We'll get you out — don't worry. Just stay where you are."

Kaylee sniffled, tears flowing. "What about Mrs. Morrison?"

"We'll check the roadblock."

She wiped her stinging eyes, and the back of her hand came away smeared black with wet soot.

"Kaylee, honey? Did you hear?"

The bomber was coming closer for

another drop. She swallowed hard and took a breath.

"I heard, Mom," she said. "I'll wait." At her feet, Sausage whined. Kaylee reached down to comfort him. "We'll wait — I've got Sausage."

"Base checks that, Kaylee. We're going to get a boat to you, okay?"

"Okay, Base." Kaylee watched through the shed window as her mom's giant, slow flying plane blocked out what was left of the sun.

"Base, Three-Seven. I'm dropping now."

Kaylee heard what sounded like thousands of tubs of water falling on rocks, then the retreating rumble of the bomber. Her mom would circle to the lake again.

A new voice crackled over the radio. "Base, this is Bird-dog One. I've been trying to get through ... too much noise. The fire is advancing along the south arm of the bay. If you want to get a boat through, you'd better get another bomber on it!"

Kaylee's stomach muscles clenched.

"Roger that, Bird-dog One. Tanker Four-Two, report."

"Base, this is Four-Two. I'm off the water for the north end of Misto. The fire is into the town. I'm working the perimeter."

"Roger that, Four-Two. Tanker One-Four report."

"Base, One-Four. I'm on the perimeter with Four-Two. The fire's crowning, and people are running in the streets — we've got to stay on the town."

"Roger that, One-Four."

The sudden quiet was deafening.

She picked the hand-mike back up. "Mom?"

"I'm with you Kaylee. I'm off the lake again on my way back." Her voice remained tight. "You stay put."

"Base, this is Bird-dog One. The mouth of the bay is closed. The fire has leapt the mouth and is into the north arm."

"Base, this is Three-Seven." Her mom was on again. "What about a chopper?"

"Negative, Three-Seven. The choppers are bucketing right now. We'll get one to you as soon as the town is stabilized. You stay on target."

"Base, that's no good!" Mom sounded upset, and Kaylee started crying again. "The fire is everywhere. We've got to do something now — that's my daughter down there!" Her voice broke.

"Stay calm, Three-Seven. We're working on it."

Kaylee looked out the shed window. Sooty smoke hemmed her in. Her mom's floatplane was bobbing violently at the end of its tether off the dock. If only her dad were there. She could almost see him put down the radio mike and shrug. He would laugh and say, "It's time for us to get outa town!"

The fear that had kept her upright now buckled her knees. She pressed her cheek into the sandy floorboards, feeling where one board met with the next. She closed her eyes wishing the crack were a doorway to some other place, imagining if she could just squeeze through she'd be safe.

Why was she here all alone? Why did Mom have to be flying, and why did Dad have to be ... gone?

There, trapped in that shed, in her desperation and her grief, the wall she had built between truth and hope splintered and fell like the blazing tree in front of Mrs. Morrison's house. Dad wasn't coming back. He wasn't on another island, and he wasn't going to fly her out of here. He was gone. She raised herself, curling her knees to her chest, hugging them. He died. Rocking back and forth, she sobbed, her tears falling to the gritty floor.

After a time, she noticed Sausage licking the soot and salty tears from her cheeks. Tuning the world back in, she heard the staccato bursts of pilot updates on the King radio and the steady drone of aircraft outside. Through all the noise she could hear the floatplane bobbing at the end of the dock.

The floatplane! She took a deep breath, stood and pressed the mike.

"Mom." Her voice caught in her throat. She cleared it and tried again, pressing the mike lever firmly. "Mom, I have an idea."

She had an idea all right. One of the scariest she'd ever had, but it was her best chance. Maybe her only chance.

"Kaylee, I'm here. What is it, hon?"

"I can take the Cessna to the middle of the bay. I'll be safe there. I'll wait out the fire."

For a moment the radio was silent.

"Yes, Kaylee." Her mom sounded hopeful. "That's a good idea. Listen. You get out to the plane now and tune up this frequency. Can you do that, honey?"

"Okay, Mom. I'm going now." She dropped the radio. As she called Sausage to follow her out of the shed she could hear: "Copy, Base?" from her mom, and "Roger that," from Base.

She pounded down the dock with Sausage, sidled across the pontoon, and crawled up into the cockpit of the Cessna. She turned on the radio, tuned it to the fire-radio frequency, and pulled on the headset. "Mom?" she called.

"I'm here, Kaylee."

"I'm in the plane, Mom. I'm going to untie it now and get back in"

"Okay, Kaylee. Just flip the knot like I showed you, and call me when you're back."

Kaylee climbed back down on the pontoon.

"Come on, Sausage." She was on her knees on the bobbing pontoon, hand out to her friend. Sausage whined, looked down at the water, backed up, bowed with his bum in the air and barked.

"Come ON, Sausage!" Kaylee called again. Sausage sat, thumping his tail. Kaylee looked to the shore. There was no time! She wished she had some food to coax him with.

Sausage whined at her.

"Okay, Sausage." Kaylee put her hand in her shorts pocket, and wiggled her fingers. "You want a treat, boy?" Sausage tilted his head and watched her hand. "Come on, boy — you want the biscuit, you come here!" She snapped the fingers on her other hand and waited. He stood, wagging his tail. Kaylee held her breath as Sausage touched one foot to the edge of the pontoon, then the other.

The pontoon bobbed wildly as Sausage leapt into Kaylee's arms. Kaylee hugged him tightly, lying flat so as not to slip off the pontoon.

"Good boy!" she said while Sausage licked her face. Then he saw the open door of the plane and, forgetting his hesitation, wiggled out of her arms, hopped in, and lay flat between the front and back seats. Sighing with relief, Kaylee turned to unfasten the rope.

"Kaylee ..."

The call was faint. Kaylee looked to the end of the dock, and blinked in shock.

"Mrs. Morrison!" Leaping onto the dock, she raced toward her neighbor, feet hammering the faded wood.

Mrs. Morrison's normally flamboyant clothes were torn and black with soot. She was hanging onto a corner of the shed, struggling to stay standing. Kaylee reached her just as she started to crumple toward the ground.

"Oh Kaylee ... " she gasped, leaning heavily. "There you are, dear. I'm so glad you're all right."

"What happened, Mrs. Morrison?" Kaylee cried. "I thought you left!"

"Spot left, dear. We fell, and his cage

popped open. He just … ran off. I tried to find him." Her eyes clouded.

Kaylee looked to shore. The lane beyond her house was once again a wall of flame and smoke. How had Mrs. Morrison come through that?

"Come with me, Mrs. Morrison. We'll be okay."

They limped down the dock. Behind them the fire roared like a freight train. Kaylee helped Mrs. Morrison into the Cessna. She was wobbly and leaned heavily on Kaylee as she climbed into a back seat. Once settled, she slumped against the window, eyes closed.

"Mrs. Morrison … are you okay?" Mrs. Morrison was ashen beneath the soot smeared on her skin.

"Oh … I'm fine dear, "she said weakly. "Just tired …"

Kaylee fastened Mrs. Morrison's seat belt and secured the door.

"Okay, Mom, I'm back. I've got Mrs.

Morrison with me."

"Mrs. Morrison?" Her mom sounded worried again. "Where did she come from?"

"From the woods, Mom. She's pretty banged up." Kaylee glanced over her shoulder. "Mrs. Morrison?" She waited. "Mom, I think she's passed out."

There was a brief pause.

"Don't worry, Kaylee. We're going to get you out of this — all of you. Are you ready?"

"I've started the plane, and it's untied." The engine's thrum vibrated through her. She was starting to feel good about her plan. "You did remember to refuel this thing, right?"

"Why, Kaylee Marie!" Kaylee could hear the smile in her mother's voice. "You're starting to sound like a pro."

"Three-Seven, this is Base. Get her out there, then switch to frequency one-three-zero-decimal-three-zero. We'll monitor you there — let's keep this main channel open."

"Roger that, Base. Okay, Kaylee, you remember this don't you? Yoke and throttle, that's all."

"Roger, Mom, yoke and throttle." Kaylee grinned. She felt kind of funny using pilot talk. She could hear her mom's bomber overhead as she pushed the throttle forward to get the plane moving. She turned toward the center of the bay with the yoke or steering column. Each of the plane's pontoons had a small rudder like a boat, and they were connected to the yoke. No sweat.

"That's good, Kaylee. Only, you're going to have to pick it up a bit — the water's pretty choppy. Push the throttle a little more. Okay, honey?"

"Roger, Mom," she said, pushing the throttle forward again, increasing the power. She felt good — in control. None of the usual fluttering in her stomach, she noticed with surprise.

"Okay, Base. We're going to go rifle

frequency now," her mom said.

"Roger that, Three-Seven. Changing to one-three-zero-decimal-three-zero."

"Kaylee, change your frequency now to onc-three-zero-decimal-three-zero. You got that?"

"Yeah Mom. one-three-zero-decimal-three-zero," she repeated, just as she had heard her mom do many times before when asked to change frequencies. She flipped the numbers around the dial quickly. When the right ones were lined up neatly, she pressed her mike again.

"Mom, this is Kaylee. I'm on one-three-zero-decimal-three-zero, and approaching the middle of the bay."

"Roger that, Kaylee. I'm proud of you, hon." Her mom sounded kind of choked. "With this wind you're going to have to circle a bit. Keep your speed above the chop of the water. You'll be fi ... "

Boom!

An explosion rocked the bay.

"Mom!" Kaylee screamed.

Chapter Twelve

Overhead, the bomber veered sharply away from the bay and the flying debris. Kaylee screamed again and ducked as something large and flat hit the windshield, blocking her view.

She had let go of the throttle in her panic and was drifting, bobbing in the wind and rough water. The windshield was mostly blocked by what looked like a navy and red patchwork quilt. She peered out her right side window — flames and smoke. Where moments ago a cedar lodge had nestled on the shore, now there was nothing.

She checked the back seat. Mrs. Morrison was now slumped forward against the shoulder harness, her chin nodding toward her chest. Sausage was calm but alert on the floor.

"Kaylee!" Mom shouted through the radio. "Kaylee ... answer me, honey! Are you okay?"

The quilt fell away from the windshield and sank into the lake. Kaylee pressed the mike. "I'm here, Mom," she said breathlessly. "What happened?"

"It was the fire, Kaylee. The lodge went fast — looks like the roof blew right off."

"That can happen?"

"It just did, Kaylee." There was a pause on the frequency. Her mom had stopped speaking, but was holding her mike open. She wasn't finished yet. "Kaylee, honey ... Kaylee ... this doesn't look too good."

Kaylee had pushed the throttle forward again and was moving. "What do you mean, Mom? The plane is fine. I'm worried about Mrs. Morrison, though."

Her mother didn't respond for a moment.

"Kaylee, the debris from that explosion scattered pretty far. And that was just a building."

Shards of ice ran through Kaylee's veins as she realized what her mother was trying to say. The fuel tanks! Every house along Booker Bay had its own large propane tank, and the small marina had two even larger tanks with diesel fuel.

"The fuel tanks, Mom? Is the fire going to get them?"

"Yes, Kaylee. The fire is everywhere. There's not much time before everything on shore goes."

Kaylee swallowed hard. They were sitting ducks.

"This may get bad, Kaylee. How's Mrs. Morrison?"

"She's still passed out, Mom." She reached

back and pushed her passenger gently toward the window. She didn't wake.

"Keep the side windows shut and hang tight ..." Her mother's voice was faint. Clearly she didn't think the bay was a good place for Kaylee to be.

Kaylee thought hard. The mouth of the bay was flamed in. She could not get through the narrow channel that led to Misto Lake. She could not return to shore. The plane could be hit in another explosion. It could sink. And no one could get to her to help.

She did have one chance.

The terrifying idea came to her, just as a great warmth washed over her.

I'm here, Kaylee.

She felt the words, rather than heard them. She looked to the right hand seat. No one was there, yet she could feel her father smiling tenderly at her. Comforting her. Reassuring her.

You can do it, honey.

As suddenly as the image had come to her, it faded. The warmth and reassurance remained.

Kaylee's heart beat hard in her chest as she turned and pressed the mike again. "I know what to do, Mom." She licked her lips and swallowed. "I'm going to take it over the trees and land it at the water base in town."

Silence.

"Did you hear me, Mom?"

"Kaylee ... " Her mom recovered quickly. "Kaylee, don't ... You can't fly the plane."

"Why not?" As desperate as she was feeling, she still felt stung. "You've told me over and over and over again how safe it is ... how there's nothing to it! Ever since I started sitting in the front with you, you've shown me how this works!"

"I know, Kaylee ... but watching is different from doing. I'm not there with you now. You have to stay put."

"But you ARE here with me now!"

Kaylee shouted, tears stinging her eyes once more. She blinked, took a breath and looked again to the seat beside her. A feeling of certainty enveloped her. "I'm not alone," she said calmly.

Silence again. In her mind's eye, Kaylee could see clearly each of the steps her mother took for take off.

She was at the center of the lake. Determined, she turned the floatplane around so that it was facing back into the wind. Butterflies stirred in her stomach. Her heart pounded against her chest. She breathed in deeply, let her breath out in a slow, steady stream, and pressed the mike button.

"I'm doing this, Mom," she said grimly. "It's our only chance."

With her right hand she reached down between the two front seats. "I'm taking the flaps down two notches — that's what you always do."

"Okay, Kaylee." Her Mom's voice was tight again, not angry, just ... controlled.

"I'm here with you, honey. You've got it pointed the right way, and your path is clear. I can't see any of the debris from the lodge in your path. Are you ready?"

"I'm ready, Mom." Cool confidence settled on Kaylee's brow, seeping downward through her neck and shoulders. "I'm pushing the throttle all the way forward now." The engine whined to a high pitch as the plane started forward, slushing heavily through the water.

"Good girl, Kaylee. Keep your nose up — pull on the yoke just a bit."

"I know, Mom." Kaylee held her hands steady on the yoke. Her back teeth vibrated with the engine as the shore rushed closer.

Out of the corner of her eye, she saw Sausage jump into the right seat, launching his front paws against the indicator panel. She stole a sideways glance and smiled.

Sausage had his mouth open, his tongue lolling to the side, as if he were laughing.

"Your speed looks good, Kaylee. Your

floats are up out of the water now ..."

The dragging feeling of wading through water disappeared, and Kaylee felt herself skimming the bay. Her pulse was racing. Rice Crispies snap-crackled through her veins.

"Keep pushing forward on the yoke, Kaylee. Steady. You're doing fine." Her mom's voice was level and calm. Kaylee followed her cues as she got closer to shore.

"Okay, you're good, honey. This is it. Steady now ... pull back a bit. You're ready to fly."

Kaylee pulled on the yoke as her mother told her, as she had seen so many times before. She was off! She was in the air!

"Woo-hoo!" she whooped, hands steady on the yoke. Sausage barked a cheer.

"You did it, Kaylee! Good girl!" Her mother's voice was like a hug. "Level off now. We'll get you to town."

"Roger, Mom."

Flying was a piece of cake, Kaylee thought. And it felt good! Maybe it was in her blood, after all.

She glanced to her right as Sausage settled himself into the seat. Had she imagined it? No. Her father had come to her when she needed him most. Maybe he had been with her all along: every day, every scrape, every path in the forest, every fallen tear.

"Okay, Mom ... now I'll bring the flaps back up."

"Never mind that, Kaylee," her mom said quickly. "You're going to land right away — the flaps won't really matter. Just hold on tight to the yoke. With the flaps down it'll pull a bit, but it's one less thing for you to worry about."

Kaylee glanced down at Booker Bay, searching for her home, but it was hidden under a blanket of smoke. She flew over the mouth of the bay, out of the smoke toward the main body of the lake.

"Keep it going, Kaylee. We need to get you out far enough so you can turn around and head back into the wind for landing." Her mom sounded calm, like she was enjoying an outing. "Look out your right window, honey."

Kaylee glanced right and saw her mom's bomber flying level with her, about as far away as the length of a soccer field. She waved, and her mom waved back.

"You're flying like you were born to do this, Kaylee. Okay, eyes forward now. Left turn ... nice and gentle ... turn it in so you're lined up to land at the water base. You'll see it. And I'll be right behind you."

Kaylee did as she was told. As she turned she saw the lake glistening at an angle below her.

"That's great Kaylee ... perfect."

A small crowd had gathered at the dock, along with an emergency truck from the hospital, and two or three people in

speedboats. The familiar knot began to wind in the pit of her stomach. "Mom ... what's with the flashing lights?"

"Don't worry about it," Mom soothed. "You're fine. I told Base about Mrs. Morrison. The boats are going to meet you after you land."

Kaylee checked the backseat. Mrs. Morrison hadn't moved.

"Watch yourself, Kaylee. I want you to pull back slowly on the throttle. Bring her in nice and smooth."

Kaylee forgot about the waiting crowd and started into her landing, remembering every step, seeing her mother's — and her father's — firm and steady hand at the controls.

She had left her flaps down as her mother had told her, so her speed was already good and slow.

"You're doing great, hon. Nice and steady ... "

She was close enough to see the chop

on the water now.

"Almost there ..."

She was almost down to rooftop level.

"Nose up now ... pull back just a bit on the yoke ... "

She was doing it!

"Get ready to pull back all the way when you're on the water, Kaylee."

She was landing!

"Steady ..."

The floats slapped the water, and she pulled back all the way. Startled, she realized she was back in the air! Without thinking, she pushed forward again and cut the power.

"Kaylee!" her mother screamed, as Kaylee's head jerked forward and hit the yoke. The world jiggled and sucked into black.

Chapter Thirteen

Kaylee opened her eyes to sunshine streaming through her open window, chasing shadows from corners. She must have dozed off in her chair. At the far end of her hospital room her mother was busy at her bed tucking a few brand new items of clothing into an overnight bag.

"Is it time to go, Mom?"

"Just about, honey," her mom answered, zipping up the bag. She moved across the room and sat in the chair opposite Kaylee. "How are you feeling?" she asked gently.

"Okay, I guess," Kaylee said, absent-mindedly running her fingers along the sling on her right arm. "Better than Mrs. Morrison. Guess I'm not much of a pilot after all."

Her mom tossed her head and laughed. "Why, Kaylee Marie! Not much of a pilot? Do you have any idea how proud I am of you? Or how scared I was for you, and how much you surprised me?" She reached over and tousled Kaylee's bangs, careful not to touch the purple goose egg on her forehead. "I told you you're a natural, and I meant it."

"I messed up the landing, though."

"You didn't mess anything up! Flying is easy, honey — it's the take-offs and landings that are tricky. You just landed hard — real hard — but under the circumstances it was pretty wonderful anyway."

Kaylee sighed. After her hard landing, she had been knocked out cold. One of the floatplane's pontoons had bent and the plane had started to sink. Three guys on speedboats, she didn't know who, had raced over and hauled Kaylee and Mrs. Morrison out to the waiting emergency truck. Sausage had needed a lot of coaxing to leave the plane, but he went too, eventually.

By late evening the fire had been beaten back. All through the night she and her mom sat whispering in her darkened hospital room, listening to bulldozers rumble, knocking over trees, creating a firebreak between the town and the woods. By morning, the main body of the fire was snuffed, though still smoldering. The town — most of it — had been spared.

Kaylee looked up at her mom. "So, what do we do now?"

"Well, I guess we have a choice. Some of our neighbors, Jack included, have decided to camp for the summer. We could join them, or we could stay in the motel I've booked us into. What would you like to do?"

Kaylee liked nothing more than camping, spending her days hiking and canoeing, but today the idea didn't cheer her. The fire had destroyed each and every house at Booker Bay. She shuddered. It could have destroyed her too. By ignoring their map code and not staying in Red Sector where she had pinned the feather, she had put herself in great danger. She tried not to think about what might have happened if she hadn't stumbled upon the hydro line.

"I don't know, Mom."

She remembered how Dad had come to her out on the Bay. He had been with her in the forest too, she realized. She sighed, a tear spilling from her eye. In her heart she knew that, in a way, he would always be there for her. Knowing that didn't stop her from being sad, though. She was letting go of something she'd been holding tight for a very long time.

"Hey ... Kaylee." Her mother reached over, and pinched the tear with her fingertips. "Think how much we have to be thankful for. Everyone made it out okay. Who knows what would have happened to Mrs. Morrison if you hadn't gone back for Sausage?"

"I miss Sausage. When can I see him, Mom?"

"Right away — he's waiting in the truck. It was nice of Jack to look after him overnight."

"Yeah. Tell him thanks for me, okay?"

"You can tell him yourself!" Mom stood, slinging the small bag over her shoulder. "He's just down the hall with Mrs. Morrison."

Kaylee looked down at her knees. She had to face Mrs. Morrison sometime, but what was she going to say? Her neighbor would give her an earful for sure. When Mrs. Morrison climbed into the plane, she didn't know Kaylee was going to fly it. What if they had crashed, and Mrs. Morrison had been hurt real bad or killed?

Mom stood in the doorway. "Would you like to stop in and see them?"

Kaylee followed her mom out the door, summoning her courage. She had fought her way out of a burning forest and flown an airplane; surely she could face Mrs. Morrison. She just wasn't looking forward to it.

They walked along the lemon yellow center-line of the hospital corridor, and around a corner. Jack stepped through an open door into the hall.

"Kaylee!" Jack took two giant steps over to her, folding her in a big hug. "I was just coming to see you — how are you?"

"I'm okay, Jack. Thanks for taking care of Sausage."

Jack nodded and smiled. They were lucky to have a friend like Jack, always there when they needed him, always looking out for her. She swallowed and hung her head. "I'm sorry I didn't stay with you at the highway, Jack."

Jack glanced at her mom. "Seems to me that's something you and your mom can talk about later. I'm just glad you're okay. I'm glad we're all okay."

"How's Mrs. Morrison?"

"Tough — very tough! The doctor said he wanted to keep her here for one more night on account of all the smoke she took in. She complained pretty loudly at first, but the staff let me bring her some company. She's happy now."

Kaylee peeked around the corner, and spied Mrs. Morrison cooing at a beast locked behind a carry-kennel door. The beast looked very cranky.

"Spot! Jack, you found him!"

"He found me. When you weren't in the truck I went looking for you. An RCMP officer stopped me from going back down the lane — said you were waiting out the fire in your mom's plane." He shook his head. "Right then Spot launched himself at me from the woods. He's a bit singed.

More insulted at being shut in that cage than anything, I think."

Kaylee's eyes clouded with tears of relief. They were all okay. That really was all that mattered. She took a deep breath, and walked into the room. "Mrs. Morrison?"

"Oh hello, dear!" Mrs. Morrison sang out. "I hear we went for a bit of a ride. Sorry I missed it. Maybe you can take me up another time."

Kaylee searched her face. Was she kidding? Mrs. Morrison threw back her head and laughed. "Kaylee, my dear, you're much too young to walk around with such a frown on your face. Be thankful. Be happy!" She turned back to the cage, and began singing to Spot — something about a cat coming back.

Kaylee looked back at Jack and her mom. They were smiling. "Come on Kaylee," her mom said. "You've got your own friend waiting in the truck. See you later, Mrs. Morrison."

"Goodbye, my dears."

They left Jack with Mrs. Morrison and continued toward the reception area.

"Tell you what," Mom said. "We'll go to the motel for now and decide later if we want to camp with the others. We've got some things to think about."

Kaylee waved goodbye to one of the nurses as they pushed open the big double glass doors to the waiting day. She glanced up at her mother curiously. "Like what?"

"My classes are finished, Kaylee. The house is gone ... maybe we'd like to settle somewhere else. With the upgrades I took, I could apply for a supervisory position anywhere."

"If you're a supervisor, does that mean you'll be home more?"

"I'll be home so much, you'll get sick of me! I still have a job to do this fire season, but we have lots to think about for next year." She pointed ahead. "Here's someone happy to see you ..."

"Sausage!"

At the sound of their voices, Sausage sprang from his resting place on the front seat, and whined wildly, scrabbling to climb through the half open window.

"Easy boy!" Kaylee laughed and climbed into the truck. She had to turn her sore arm away as Sausage snuffled into her, licking her face and trying his best to crawl into her lap. Kaylee hugged him, burying her face in the ruff of his neck. "Settle down boy," she said. "I missed you too."

Mom started the big truck engine.

"Mom, can we go home?"

Her mother paused briefly before putting the truck in gear. "I'm guessing you're not talking about the motel."

"No." She rubbed gently behind her hound dog's ears. "Can we go to Booker Bay first?"

"It's not very pretty, honey," her mother said softly, brows furrowed. "It's spooky … there's nothing left."

"That's okay. Please, Mom?" she pleaded. "I just need to see it."

Her mom glanced over at her, hesitating. "Okay. Let's go." Her smile was more than part grimace.

Driving along the highway, Kaylee could see the charred path of the wild fire. The wind had pushed it in a straight line from the west across the highway. She smiled briefly as they passed the Smokey the Bear Fire Hazard Warning, still intact. The arrow indicated a high hazard, and the grass and shrubs below the sign were burnt and black. No kidding. As they got closer to Booker Bay, small areas within the burnt woods still spewed smoke. Here and there ground crews worked with shovels, putting out "hot spots." The truck turned off the access road onto what used to be their lane.

It was awful, more like haunted woods in a ghost story than the boreal forest she had hiked and loved. What used to be dense and wild were now a few charred sticks. The houses that once nestled side by side along the bay had been incinerated. The foundations stood exposed, along with the propane tanks that had fuelled the homes.

"I guess the fuel tanks were okay," Kaylee said bleakly.

"Looks like it, honey."

Kaylee watched her mother as she stopped the truck and got out. She walked toward the water, neck and shoulders stiff. With a start, Kaylee realized this must be as difficult for Mom as it was for her. She followed her to the edge of the lake.

"We built this place ourselves, you know," Mom whispered, staring far out over the water.

"Did it take a long time?" Kaylee reached for her mother's hand.

"Most of a summer, I guess."

Kaylee took a deep breath, "You know what, Mom?" Her mother continued to gaze at the lake. "When I was in the plane,

I realized that Dad is still with us." A weight seemed to lift as she spoke. "He always will be."

Mom turned, tearful, but smiling. They both stood silent for a long moment.

"Mom?" Kaylee went on. "I know where I'd like us to go."

"You mean camping, honey?"

"No ... I mean after this fire season. I want to go back to the island."

Her mom sighed, turning back to the water. "Kaylee, we've been through this again and again."

"No, it's okay, Mom." Kaylee reached for her mother's hand. "Really. I know Dad's not waiting for us there. Only I guess he is, kind of. Not for us to find him ... but maybe to say goodbye. The island was Dad's home as much as this place, and this place is gone. I just want to feel close one more time."

Kaylee watched as her mother struggled with her thoughts. "Maybe it's time," she said finally. "Nana and Papa would like us to come. Maybe St. Lucia is a good place to figure out where we want to go next. Do you mean it ... about saying goodbye, I mean?"

"Yeah." She watched a loon take off, a black-tipped, speckled dart aiming for the sun, water dropping from her white underbelly as she left the bay behind. You'd be loony to stay, she thought. Nothing here but burned up sticks. And memories. She sighed.

She barely heard her mother when she spoke. "You're a lot braver than I am, Kaylee."

As the loon flew out of sight beyond the blackened forest, Kaylee looked sideways at her mother. "Can I fly us there?" She grinned mischievously, as her mom raised her eyebrows at her.

"So this is how it's going to be, is it?" She snorted. "Every time you want to go somewhere you're going to ask for the airplane keys?"

"Well, you know, Mom," Kaylee said, giggling, "I think I've outgrown my bike!"

"What bike?" Mother and daughter were both laughing loudly now, silly-tears streaming down their cheeks. "I don't see any bike around here!"

A deep bark from the truck made them jump. Sausage was leaning out the open window, head cocked sharply to one side.

Kaylee took a deep happy breath and wiped her cheeks dry with her left hand, still careful of her other arm in its sling. "I think Sausage wants to know where his bed is. Do you think he'll like sleeping on a beach?"

Anita Daher has been writing about forest fires ever since her family and their dog, Copper, aka Sausage, had to be evacuated when a forest fire outside La Ronge, Saskatchewan, almost took their home. Aviation goes way back in her family. Her grandfather was a navigator during the Second World War, while she herself has worked as a radio operator in small airports. Like Kaylee, Anita still gets knots in her stomach when she has to fly. She now lives with her family in Sault Ste. Marie, Ontario.